DATE DUE

DEC 0 6 2004	
NOV 2 8 2005	
NOV 1 3 2006	
NOV 1 1 2008	
DEC 0 1 2008	
NOV 2 1 2011	
NOV 2 6 2012	
NOV 1 9 2014	

DEMCO, INC. 38-2931

HILLTOP SCHOOL LIBRARY

The Hopi

by Allison Lassieur

Consultants:
Hopi Literacy Project
Bureau of Applied Research in Anthropology
University of Arizona

Bridgestone Books
an imprint of Capstone Press
Mankato, Minnesota

Bridgestone Books are published by Capstone Press
151 Good Counsel Drive, P.O. Box 669, Mankato, Minnesota 56002
http://www.capstone-press.com

Copyright © 2002 Capstone Press. All rights reserved.
No part of this book may be reproduced without written permission from the publisher.
The publisher takes no responsibility for the use of any of the materials
or methods described in this book, nor for the products thereof.
Printed in the United States of America.

Library of Congress Cataloging-in-Publication Data
Lassieur, Allison.
　　The Hopi / by Allison Lassieur.
　　p. cm.—(Native peoples)
　　Includes bibliographical references and index.
　　Summary: Provides an overview of the past and present lives of the Hopi, covering their daily life, customs and beliefs, government, and more.
　　ISBN 0-7368-1102-8
　　1. Hopi Indians—Juvenile literature. [1. Hopi Indians. 2. Indians of North America—Arizona.] I. Title. II. Series.
E99.H7 L37 2002
979.1'0049745—dc21　　　　　　　　　　　　　　　　　　　　　　　　2001005174

Editorial Credits
Tom Adamson, editor; Karen Risch, product planning editor; Timothy Halldin, cover
　　and interior layout designer; Heidi Meyer, production designer and interior illustrator;
　　Alta Schaffer, photo researcher

Photo Credits
Owen Seumptewa, 16
Susanne Page, cover, 6, 8 (both), 10, 12, 14, 18, 20

1 2 3 4 5 6 07 06 05 04 03 02

Table of Contents

Map 4
Fast Facts 5

Hopi History 7
Homes, Food, and Clothing 9
Clans 11
The Hopi Family 13
Farming 15
Religion 17
How the Hopi Reached This World 19
Hopi Government 21

Hands On: Hopi Language 22
Words to Know 23
Read More 23
Useful Addresses 24
Internet Sites 24
Index 24

The Hopi always have lived in northeastern Arizona near the Grand Canyon. The Hopi reservation is part of their traditional lands. Both the Hopi and Navajo use the area shown in blue on the map.

Fast Facts

The Hopi (HOH-pee) are a Pueblo Indian tribe. They have lived in the deserts of the southwestern United States for hundreds of years. The Hopi are proud of their past. These facts tell about Hopi history.

Homes: The Hopi lived in buildings made of stone and natural clay. Each tall, box-shaped home had many rooms. Hopi families built their homes close together in small villages.

Food: Hopi farmers grew food such as corn and squash. Women gathered seeds and fruits. Men hunted wild animals such as rabbit and antelope.

Clothing: Long ago, the Hopi wore clothing made of fur or animal skins. Later, men dressed in shirts and pants made from woven cotton. Women wore cotton or wool dresses called *mantas*.

Language: The Hopi language is a Uto-Aztecan language. Southwestern Indian tribes such as Hopi, Yaqui, and O'odham speak languages from this group.

Villages

The Hopi have lived on their land for hundreds of years. Hopi people have lived in the village of Oraibi for at least 850 years. Oraibi is the oldest continuously inhabited American Indian village in the United States.

There are several other small villages on the Hopi reservation. Some of them are on top of mesas. These high mountains have steep sides and a flat top. The village in this photo is called Walpi.

Hopi History

In 1540, Spanish explorer Pedro de Tovar met the Hopi people. He was the first European to see the Hopi. Spanish soldiers later moved into Hopi lands. Later, priests came to Hopi lands. These religious leaders wanted the Hopi to believe in Christianity. Most Hopi did not want to give up their traditional beliefs.

The Hopi and other Pueblo tribes wanted the Spanish to leave. In 1680, the Hopi and Pueblo tribes led the Pueblo Revolt. They defeated the priests and soldiers. The Spanish left the Hopi alone after that battle.

In the 1800s, the Navajo tried to take Hopi lands. U.S. President Chester Arthur created the Hopi reservation in 1882. This act was supposed to stop the Navajo from taking more land. But the Navajo did not stop. In 1974, a law called the Navajo-Hopi Land Settlement Act gave some land back to the Hopi. Today, the Hopi and the Navajo still do not agree about who should use the land.

Long ago, girls who were old enough to marry wore their hair in whorls. Each large whorl was on one side of the head. Today, some young women wear their hair in whorls for ceremonies.

Homes, Food, and Clothing

The Hopi live in large stone houses. A house might be two or three stories high. The walls are plastered on the inside and outside with natural clay. A Hopi village is made of many houses built around an open area called a *kiisonvi*. The Hopi have lived in these houses for hundreds of years.

The Hopi people's food comes from the high desert where they live. Farmers grow corn, squash, and beans. Long ago, men hunted animals such as antelope, deer, and rabbit. Women gathered berries, nuts, and seeds. The Hopi still make a rolled, flat bread called *piiki* out of blue corn flour.

The Hopi were one of the only tribes to grow cotton for clothing. Men wore cotton shirts and pants. Women wore black cotton dresses.

The Hopi people's box-shaped homes are made with stone and natural clay.

Clans

The word Hopi comes from a longer word in the Hopi language, *Hopisinom*. It means "people who follow the Hopi way of life."

The Hopi people are divided into about 34 clans. Each clan is made up of many families. The Bear Clan, Eagle Clan, Badger Clan, and Spider Clan are some of the clans.

Members of the same clan sometimes live in different villages. Clan members from one village are welcome in their clan members' homes in another village.

Each Hopi clan has its own history and traditional stories. Every clan is responsible for holding ceremonies and for keeping sacred objects. The Hopi are taught to take care of all people and treat them with respect.

The Buffalo Dance is one ceremony that takes place on the Hopi reservation.

The Hopi Family

Families are important to the Hopi. Every family in a clan shares the clan's traditions.

The children in a family belong to the mother's clan. Aunts and uncles on the mother's side are just as important as parents. They teach the children the traditions of their clan.

The Hopi had many marriage customs. Today, some Hopi get married in a church. But most Hopi still practice traditional customs.

Two people from the same clan cannot get married. A bride might stay with the groom's family for several days. She cooks meals to show that she can care for her new husband. In a special ceremony, the groom's parents might wash the couple's hair. They use suds from the roots of the yucca plant.

These women are making a sweet corn flour pudding called *pik'ami*.

Farming

Farming is the main part of Hopi culture and history. Each village has its own lands. Each clan in the village has a part of the land. The women in the clans control the use of the land. Men plant crops and take care of the fields. Farming is still important to the Hopi. It teaches young Hopi about the customs and beliefs of their people.

Hopi lands get very little rain. It is difficult to grow crops on the land. Melting snow from nearby mountains flows to the desert. Winter and spring rains also soak the fields where the Hopi grow crops.

The Hopi plant fields at the mouths of arroyos. These deep ditches carry water from melting mountain snow and seasonal rains. The water carries dirt. This soil settles where the arroyos spread out onto flat land. The Hopi use this water and soil to grow their crops. Planting crops in these areas is called flood plain farming.

Hopi men take care of the fields. But the women in each clan control the use of the land.

Religion

Religion is a large part of Hopi culture and history. Most Hopi follow their traditional religion.

The Hopi believe that the universe was made into four worlds. The world we live in today is the Fourth World. The Hopi believe that they climbed into this world through a hatchway called the *sipaapuni*.

The Hopi also believe in spirits called *katsinas*. *Katsinas* live in the spirit world. They are kind and generous to the Hopi. *Katsinas* come to Hopi land at a certain time each year. They bring gifts of rain and food. They perform dances for the people. These dances help the Hopi feel good about their lives.

All Hopi villages have a ceremonial place called a *kiva*. These rectangular rooms are underground. People climb down a ladder into a *kiva* through a hatchway in the roof. The Hopi hold religious ceremonies in their *kivas*.

Spirits called *katsinas* bring dolls that are made to look like them. The *katsina* dolls usually are given to girls.

How the Hopi Reached This World

In the beginning, everything was dark. Then the Sun was created. The Moon and the stars were created next. The people grew strong.

In the world before this one, people began to fight among themselves. One day, the leaders decided to plant a bamboo tree for the good people to climb into this world. The tree grew tall enough to reach up into the next world. They climbed up inside the bamboo to come to this world. This is the world where people live today.

The place where they came out is called the *sipaapuni*. The Hopi believe that the *sipaapuni* still exists. It is in the Grand Canyon. This place is sacred to the Hopi.

The Hopi people mark their world with the Four Directions. This artwork shows the Four Directions of the Hopi world.

Hopi Government

Each Hopi village had its own leaders. The leaders usually came from the clan that started the village. These leaders held ceremonies and advised people in the village.

Today, Hopi villages still have their own governments. Most villages follow a traditional system of leadership for religious practices. A *kikmongwi* supports the village in religious matters. Most villages also have a Community Service Administrator. This person works with the Hopi Tribal Council and with the Hopi people in the villages.

All villages also are governed by the Hopi Tribal Council. Most villages have representatives on the Tribal Council. The Council is led by a Chairman. The Tribal Council makes modern laws for the tribe.

The Hopi Tribal Council makes modern laws for the tribe.

Hands On: Hopi Language

The Hopi want to preserve their language. Try to say these words and phrases from the Hopi language.

askwali	(ahss-kwah-lee)	thank you (said by females)
kwakwha	(kwahk-ha)	thank you (said by males)
kwa'a	(kwa-ah)	grandpa
so'o	(soh-oh)	grandma
pew'i	(peoo-ee)*	come here
taawa	(tahh-wah)*	sun
muuyaw	(meu-yow)	moon
soohu	(sohh-hu)	star
is ali	(iss ah-lee)	it tastes great!

The phrase "is ali" is similar to "mmm good!" in English.

These are the words used for numbers in counting.

sùukya'	(seu-kyah)	one
lööyö'	(leuu-yeu)	two
paayo'	(pahh-yoh)*	three
naalöyö'	(nahh-leu-yeu)	four
tsivot	(tsee-vot)	five

* There is no sound in English equal to 'p' or 't' in the Hopi language. In Hopi, the 'p' and 't' sound softer than in English.

Words to Know

arroyo (uh-ROY-oh)—a deep ditch in the desert formed by running water
ceremony (SER-uh-moh-nee)—formal actions, words, or music that honor a person, an event, or a higher being
Christianity (kriss-chee-AN-uh-tee)—a religion based on the life and teachings of Jesus Christ
council (KOUN-suhl)—a group of leaders chosen to look after the interests of a community
religion (ri-LIJ-uhn)—a set of spiritual beliefs people follow
sacred (SAY-krid)—having to do with religion
tradition (truh-DISH-uhn)—a custom, idea, or belief that is passed on to younger people by older relatives

Read More

Isaacs, Sally Senzell. *Life in a Hopi Village.* Picture the Past. Chicago: Heinemann, 2001.

Kamma, Anne. *If You Lived with the Hopi.* New York: Scholastic, 1999.

Sita, Lisa. *Indians of the Southwest.* Native Americans. Milwaukee: Gareth Stevens, 2000.

Useful Addresses

Hopi Cultural Center
P.O. Box 67
Second Mesa, AZ 86043

Hopi Tribal Council
P.O. Box 123
Kykotsmovi, AZ 86039

Internet Sites

Hopi Cultural Preservation Office
http://www.nau.edu/~hcpo-p
The Hopi of the Southwest
http://www.carnegiemuseums.org/cmnh/exhibits/north-south-east-west/hopi/index.html
Hopi Tribe
http://www.hopi.nsn.us

Index

clans, 11, 13, 15, 21
cotton, 5, 9
desert, 5, 9, 15
farming, 15
food, 5, 9, 17
government, 21
Grand Canyon, 4, 19
homes, 5, 9, 11
Hopi Tribal Council, 21
katsinas, 17
kikmongwi, 21
kiva, 17
marriage, 8, 13
Navajo, 4, 7
Navajo-Hopi Land Settlement Act, 7
Pueblo Revolt, 7
religion, 7, 17, 21
sipaapuni, 17, 19
Spanish soldiers, 7
Tovar, Pedro de, 7
villages, 5, 6, 9, 11, 15, 17, 21

HILLTOP SCHOOL LIBRARY